HER HI-FI HUNK

A Beach Avenue Babes Romance

ABBY KNOX

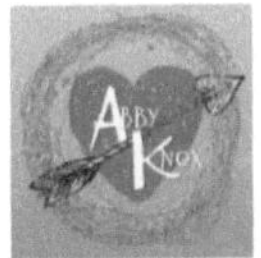

Edited by Aquila Editing

Cover Designer: Mayhem Cover Creations

Her Hi-Fi Hunk

Beach Avenue Babes, Part Two

By Abby Knox

Rock legend Jed is ready to heal the broken heart that has fueled more No. 1 hits than he can count. But although he shreds on the guitar, he's no player when it comes to women. His destiny simply isn't going to be plucked out of a line of groupies after his latest sold-out show. He is waiting until the time is right to make a play for the one he's admired from afar for years. Record store owner Dusty wonders when someone is going to put her little business on the map. Little does she realize the anonymous person who has been helping to keep her store afloat is also a guitar god, for whom women the world over swoon. Is she ready to accept her fate and all that entails?

FINE PRINT: This is a later-in-life romance for both MCs. The book begins with the hero coming out of a failed marriage. There is no cheating. The MCs do not meet in person or become romantically involved until after the hero is divorced. No cliffhanger, but this is the companion book to Her Vinyl Vixen. Each can be read as a stand-alone.

Chapter 1

D^{usty}

2004

BY THE TIME the black Suburbans begin their slow, winding ascent up the mountain, one clueless young mother at the top of the ridge is at her breaking point with commune life.

That's me. I am the clueless young mother.

"I hate broomstick skirts," I mutter as I hike up my flowing garments between my legs and stuff the hemline into my belt. "Why do the women have to wear the skirts if we have to do all the work around here?"

The tucking is essential to avoid splashing frigid water onto my clothes during the pre-dawn task of pumping water. Chores suck. But, being off-grid, hand-pumping the water is essential for cooking, drinking, washing dishes, the most basic sanitation. And occasional bathing. Oh yes, we all stink.

I miss running water. I miss hair dryers. I hate being cold. I need a hot shower. Fuck being off the grid, I think as I work at the rusty metal hand pump at the edge of the camp.

Everyone else is still asleep, and so I am the first to hear the engines. The noise is so jarring to the peaceful little fossil-fuel-free settlement.

I peek down the slope of scrubby trees and watch the imposing vehicles snaking slowly up the treacherous, narrow path. Hairs stand up on the back of my neck. Squinting, I can just make out the letters: ATF, FBI, DEA.

Shit.

Time to get the hell outta Dodge. I thought I'd have more time to stash away some more cash.

I drop the ungodly heavy buckets of water, letting the precious water spill onto the scrubby ground. *Fuck it.*

I run back to our family tent and silently grab the three most precious possessions: a duffel bag full of money, my seven-year-old daughter Zara, and a pair of eyeglasses.

The last thing on that list is chosen solely out of spite.

Who knows, maybe the glasses will turn into a little bit of windfall for Zara's benefit. If they are the real deal, I could, someday, get a crap ton of money for them on the black market.

Everything else, I leave behind. Our clothes. Zara's special blanket. Water. Everything.

"Mommy, I need my fuzzy blanket."

Zara looks pitifully up at me.

I chew on my lip anxiously for a second. We need to get gone, fast. If we leave right now, we might reach the scrabbly little town down in the valley in time to catch the first bus out this morning. But if I grab Zara and run for it,

I risked making a seven year old scream for her blanket and wake the whole camp.

I squat down to eye level with Zara. "Baby, what I have in this bag will buy you seventeen new special blankets." Actually, a lot more than seventeen.

Zara isn't hearing it. "Auntie made me that blanket."

Auntie. That could be any one of the completely random and not-blood-related women who live with us at the campground, who pass the time knitting, crocheting, weaving—and a lot of other crafty shit that I can never get the hang of.

I sigh. "Stay quiet and move fast."

I wait outside the tent while Zara goes in to fetch her blanket.

I prayed to whoever will listen that Zara remains quiet enough not to wake Walter.

Then comes the sound of the gravelly male voice. "What you doin', girlie girl?"

Shit. Walter's awake. I hold my breath and try to stay calm. I listen as Walter and Zara talk back and forth.

After what feels like a millennium, Zara exits the tent, clutching her blanket to her chest. From inside, Walter makes the all-too-familiar sound of rolling over to go back to sleep.

The two of us, mother and daughter, descend the mountain on foot, the duffel bag of cash in my left hand, Zara's hand in the other hand, and the glasses in my pocket.

Chapter 2

J^{ed}

2008

THE GOLD and purple sunset and the aroma of steaks on the grill always draws me outside without much coaxing, even when I'm in a bad mood.

Carrying my six-pack of Bud under my arm, I cross through the gate that connects my beachfront property line with that of my friendly neighbors.

Those neighbors have become great friends over the years to me and Darlene. They have even stuck with me after our recent contentious separation.

Over the span of my music career, I have seen so many couples in the business get busted up over one thing or another, it makes my head spin; and always, the couples' friends choose a side. More often than not, they choose the wife. When Darlene moved permanently into our Texas ranch last year, these neighbors stuck by me.

I can hardly blame Darlene. She is a true, old-school yellow rose of Texas and a decent guitar player in her own right. We've been sweethearts since she kicked my ass senior year in the Battle of the Bands competition back at good ol' Plano Senior High School. I'd rather not say what year. Suffice it to say, I'm fuckin' old.

Old enough that if you play my greatest hits online, YouTube will start showing you PSAs on how to recognize the signs of a stroke. Fuck that though; my blood panels are just fine.

Darlene hates life on the road and always preferred to stay in one place to raise our two boys, Nelson and Watts. On top of that, she hates California, whereas the West Coast lifestyle agrees with me. I'm always up for a bottle of Shiner and a toast to "Texas Forever," but I'm more of a barefoot beach bum than a boots and longhorns kind of fella.

The rock and roll paychecks have ensured that she and the boys never have been deprived of a single thing. But once the boys were grown and out of the house, my wife's patience wore thin. She grew tired of my schedule while I was away, and tired of my face when I was home.

I look out over the ocean and have the urge to call her. I missed her friendship, even if our marriage wasn't working.

But the truth was, I didn't know if I really wanted her company, or just the company of somebody. There's still an outside chance that she'll agree to counseling and we can work this out. I hate the thought of being alone, and I hate the thought of what the media exposure will do to her.

If our massive waterfront estate on the coast of Santa

Barbara, abutting properties of A-list celebrities and business moguls, isn't enough to keep her here, then certainly my company will not be a draw to bring her here, so there's no point in calling her right now.

If the idea of spending time on my married friends' deck makes me a little sad, it only lasts a while. Pretty soon, the beer, the view, the steaks and the conversation help me forget about my own troubles, if just for one night.

And then, something magical happens.

"Hey guys," I say, "There's this song that's been stuck in my head and I can't name it."

"Hum it," says Marti.

Neither Galen nor Marti can identify it.

We three friends go back and forth for several minutes trying to identify the tune.

Then Marti nudges Galen. "You know who would know?"

Galen laughs. "Yeah, I think I know who would know. Give her a call."

I am intrigued. "Who're you calling?"

Marti smiles and whips out her brand new iPhone 3G. "An old friend from high school. Actually, her daughter, to be precise. Total recall when it comes to music."

Galen laughs. "Yeah, she's a little scary though."

"I hate cell phones, we can just go inside and use the landline…" I slur, slightly tipsy and about to go on a rant about technology.

Marti waves me off, "You're going to need one of these before you know it. They're amazing."

I am ready to reply, but suddenly Marti has someone on the line. "Hi Dusty, it's me. Our friend here is trying to remember the name of a song and it's killing all of us. Can Zara help?"

A moment later, I'm talking on the phone to a small

girl who could not be more over this whole entire party trick. I hum a few bars.

I'm about six notes in and I hear an exasperated sigh, and then she names the song.

"That's it!" I exclaim.

"Super. Can I go now, Ma?"

I try to thank her, but the little girl's voice is replaced by that of the girl's mother, and it throws me for a loop. Not a loop, more like scrambles me like a Texas twister on steroids.

"Is that all you needed?"

Whoa.

Her voice is husky and sweet with an edge, like fine whiskey. A little burn if you're not prepared for it, but nice and warm going down. That voice cascades all the way down to my darkest corners. It reaches something in me.

My brain and my cock immediately react in tandem. I am confused by it. I am way too old to get a stiffy just from hearing a woman's voice on the phone. And too married, dammit. I chalk it up to missing my wife, who, if I'm honest, hasn't touched my dick in months.

I clear my throat. A stalling tactic to give myself a second to get my head straight. "Thank you, ma'am. You have a very smart daughter."

She chuckles and thanks me for the compliment. Her throaty laugh holds the promise of a female who could appreciate a very dirty joke.

"As you can see by her attitude, she doesn't like it when I use her for party tricks. It's fine, just more fodder for her future therapist. Have a good night."

I listen as she hangs up. She has an incredibly sexy way of saying goodnight. I didn't even have time to tell her who I was.

Maybe that's for the best. People always act differently when they realized who I am.

I briefly think about asking Marti what the story is with Dusty but decide against it. There's no way she is not married or at least seeing somebody.

Three more beers later, my curiosity gets the better of me.

"So…what's the deal with your friend Dusty?"

Marti and Galen grin at each other.

Marti sips her white wine and smirked. "Single mom. Runs a little indie record store down in Sea Grove. Why?"

"No reason."

Sea Grove. I like Sea Grove. It's a smaller, quieter, artsier, undiscovered version of Venice Beach. More chill. I've never played there, but Willie and I once scored some good shit there, back in the day. I could use some of that good shit about now. Especially now that Darlene isn't around to fuss at me about my stash.

Too bad there isn't any open dates on the tour I'm scheduled to start the next day, or I'd make a stop in Sea Grove to check out the record store.

When I stumble home that night, I phone my tour manager.

"I want to make a stop in Sea Grove after LA and before San Diego. Do a little surprise show in a bar somewhere down there."

"No can do, Big Daddy. No time."

"It'll be real quick. We can even do it at a local record store, maybe right on the boardwalk. Just me and my guitar. Wouldn't even need the crew. It would give people a huge thrill, maybe help sell more tickets."

"Buddy, you're sold out everywhere. There's nothing to gain from that."

"Except that it would make me happy."

My manager huffs. "The only way to make that happen is to blow off all the interviews and appearances in the 24 hours in between LA and San Diego. And besides that, check your contract. If you perform without your unionized crew at any time during the duration of a tour, you'll get your ass sued. More importantly, my ass will get sued. Forget about it. You're drunk, Jed. Get some sleep. Big day tomorrow, in case you forgot."

I hang up the phone and roll over on my bed. Fuckin' asshole. Still, he is covering my ass, I guess.

Besides all that, I'm down deep an old-fashioned guy. I can't go chasing tail while I'm still legally married. I mean, I can, and no one would judge me.

But personally, I can't get those marriage vows out of my head, you know? On the off chance that maybe things might work out.

And yet, the other thing I can't get out of my head is Dusty's voice.

So instead of sleeping it off, I get up and fire up my laptop.

Bingo. She has a website.

I find out the name of the store and even see an email address to place online orders.

I suddenly have the need to order the complete collection of The Who on vinyl, and I know exactly who I'm gonna buy from.

Chapter 3

D^{usty}

PRESENT DAY

THE HANDSOME BLOND hippie is more polite than the usual buskers who play in front of my record store every summer. Usually, the business owners along Beach Avenue in Sea Grove simply tolerate all the street performers, but this one is different.

This one, Kai, seems to want permission from me.

We are standing outside of my store, Vinyl Vixen, talking.

"You can play here as long as you want, as long as you play well. That's my only condition. Let's hear it."

He plays me a Willie Nelson song. Interesting choice. He seems too young to know who that is. It's good. Nice singing voice. Good playing. He's been doing this for a while.

"You can stay. Where'd you learn to play like that, by the way?"

"My aunt Jo," he says. "She raised me since I was little. Up in Oregon. She didn't have much, but she always made sure I had whatever creative outlet I wanted."

This kid has a story, and I'm gonna dig it out. "I bet she misses you," I say.

Kai doesn't even blink. "I send her half of everything I make. It's the least I can do."

Now my bullshit detector is pinging. So I share a little about myself, just to see if he takes the bait.

"Zara and I had a difficult journey early on. We came here to start our lives over, so it's no surprise to me when people come here for different reasons. Her father is a son of a bitch. I'll leave it at that. In fact, he's getting out of jail soon, from what I've heard. Hasn't stopped him from getting on social media to harass all my friends and spread misinformation. But overall I'm grateful. Zara has ten times the street smarts that I had at her age. I was pregnant and following my loser boyfriend all the way up a mountain to live off the grid when I was 21. So, street smart and book smart is a combination I definitely cannot take credit for. She got herself through college and now my baby's coming home. I can't complain."

I watch Kai carefully to see what part of my story piques his interest.

"Out of prison soon, huh? You know, I have some background in security. Just saying, if you want protection, I got you."

"You're a cop?"

He hesitates. "Former cop. For a private firm. It's complicated."

I reply, "Suppose you tell me all about that long story over coffee?"

And he does. At Zara's and my favorite coffee place, Voltaire's, Kai and I get to know each other a bit.

He's good looking, smart, has a kind but slightly troubled aura about him. He sparks a maternal feeling in me, maybe because I never had a son. It makes no sense; I've never been anything other than completely fulfilled as a mother while raising Zara.

"Something about you makes me want you to meet my daughter. Is that weird?"

Kai laughs, a little bit self-deprecatingly. At this moment, I find myself teetering close to the edge of arranging his marriage to my daughter. She needs a little bit of Kai in her impeccably ordered life.

"You would love her. She is organized on a whole other level—a dutiful little box-checker. Overachiever. Never did drugs, never fooled around. Rarely drinks. Finished school early. Never had a serious boyfriend or even a fling, that I'm aware of. I'm sure that has everything to do with not wanting to make the same mistakes I did."

Kai cocks his head thoughtfully and tells me, "I believe there are no mistakes; we all end up where we're supposed to end up. Sometimes we just…take the scenic route."

Oh, he's good. I like him. My future son-in-law.

Geez, I'd better cool it. But I have zero chill. I want this guy and Zara to meet, fall in love, get married, and give me a million grand babies tomorrow.

Looking over his thin frame, I know I'll have to fatten him up a bit first. I'm not much of a cook, but I just have this crazy urge to feed Kai a giant plate of fried chicken and mashed potatoes. Maternal instinct on overload now.

"I'm going to order a slice of Black Forest cake, and you're having one too," I say.

When I come back to the table with the cake, he gobbles it up and tells me everything. "You might not want me around your daughter at all, and I wouldn't blame you. I left Oregon because I shot a guy. My uncle. I was defending my Aunt Jo. He'd come home drunk, again. It was the last time he ever put a hand on her. Or anybody else. There was an investigation. I shot him in the back. And there was an insurance policy that my aunt benefitted from, so the cops were really suspicious of me.

The security company put me on mental health leave. Because my uncle was a retired cop, there were a few guys on the force who had it in for me. I was being followed, harassed. Eventually the security company let me go, and then it was impossible to find work anywhere. Everywhere I looked, my name was already mud. Jo encouraged me to leave and go find myself, practice my music. So that's where I'm at."

I'm stunned and I have to process all of this as I finish my cake. I also make a mental note to background-check the shit out of this guy before Zara comes home. Finally, I say, "I'm so sorry that all happened to you. But you know what? You did what you had to do. He might have killed her."

"I honestly believe he would have."

"Kai, if you want a permanent spot to play your music in front of my store, you can stay here as long as you want. Just don't tell my daughter you're an ex-cop. Because of the way we left her dad, she gets anxious around police."

Kai smiles. "I won't tell if you won't."

We clink coffee cups, and then I have an idea. "Zara likes her coffee with milk, no sugar."

Chapter 4

D usty

MY ONLY DAUGHTER is turning 21 years old today, and I can hardly believe it.

Maybe it's because I've missed her so badly while she's been away at college, but I watch Zara apply her makeup and I'm overwhelmed by this stunning young lady that I somehow made with my own body. It's true, what they say about children. They are your heart walking around outside of your body.

For the last 21 years, there has been no other love that felt as real and as strong and scary as the love I have for my kid.

I reach over and pet Zara's gorgeous dark locks.

"Want me to put some Dutch milkmaid braids in it?"

Zara, with her usual sideways smirk, declines. "Hard pass," she says. No surprise. Zara was never one for cutesy things like braids and polka dots. Zara is more of a Doc

Martens and facial piercing and heavy black eyeliner kind of girl.

I study my daughter's outfit and decide she carries off the look even better than I did back in the day. Plaid mini-skirt, boots, mesh top. Zara may be a musical trivia phenomenon across all generations, but she found her niche in early 1980s punk and never left.

And that is fine with me. She has good taste, and also the look and attitude probably kept her safe and free of bad boys throughout her teenage years.

But now that she's 21, I'm concerned that Zara has been a little too careful. A little too standoffish. A little too…unfun. Is that a word?

I'm certain she has never experienced sowing her wild oats.

Little does Zara know, my plan to change that is already in the works.

Kai is a combo meal: the perfect suitor for Zara and a protective man to have around now that Walter is getting out of prison.

And on that note, I have a phone call to make after Zara leaves for work.

"Marti! It's me. Is it OK if I come up to see you tomorrow? Walter's getting out soon and I'd like to make arrangements for something of his that I have…something he's going to come looking for."

After this conversation, I'm feeling optimistic as I go to work this morning.

First order of business is to check my email. Sure enough, there's an email with the results of a full background check on Kai. Everything he says checks out. No state or federal criminal records, here or in Oregon. Good school transcripts. Clean credit. He was a damn Eagle Scout. Literally.

I'm relieved but not surprised. After my experience with Walter, I'm pretty good at figuring out when I'm being bullshitted.

Zara is pretty intuitive, too, and she will no doubt pick up on my manipulations. She will not appreciate me interfering in her love life. Nor will she be thrilled with me taking an impromptu road trip tomorrow.

But she'll get over it.

Besides, I have a good feeling about this particular caper. There's no way they're not the perfect match. And there's no way Walter, who is probably emaciated after years in prison for weapons, drugs, and tax evasion, will get past Kai.

I glance through my other emails.

Like every Friday morning, there's an order from that guy named Jed with the P.O. Box in Santa Barbara.

He'd first emailed me through my record store's website years ago, and since then he has ordered something from me at least once a week.

Sometimes it's a rare bootleg. Other times, it's an entire discography of a certain band. Another time, he was looking for a 45 of an INXS song he lost in the '90s. Anytime there was news of a death of a famous musician, I would, within minutes, hear a bloop notifying me of a new email.

When David Bowie died, Jed and I had emailed back and forth a few times, consoling each other. Same with Leonard Cohen. Same with Prince.

Oh god. Prince! My heart still hurts.

Jed never told me much about himself, just kept the conversation focused on the music.

I always wondered why he never made a trip to the shop personally, but he said he traveled a lot for work.

This morning, there's a new email from Jed. And

maybe I'm just feeling in love with the idea of the possibility of love, but the sight of this message from him gives me a little thrill.

I should be careful: for all I know he could be trolling me. He could be a serial killer. But I doubt it. That bullshit detector never seems to ping with this guy.

"Hey, Dusty. Looking for this early hip-hop song…" he writes this morning.

I smirk. "Hey, Jed from Santa Barbara. At the risk of hurting my bottom line, but for the sake of my own curiosity, why have you never used Amazon or eBay?"

He replies: "I like the personal touch. I like you. And I have a special request. Can you bring the record to Galen and Marti's tomorrow?"

My fingers flinch away from the keyboard like I've been bitten by a snake. How does he know my friends?

And then I have to sit and think for a minute. They do live in Santa Barbara… They have mentioned they have a super-rich and reclusive neighbor who asks them to be discreet about his comings and goings… These email orders started coming in shortly after that time they put Zara on the phone with their friend, though at the time they never said he was the neighbor… And every time I've visited them, they mentioned that their neighbor is away for work.

Is it possible this is that guy from the phone call years ago? That's crazy.

I cannot decide how I feel about this right now. Have I been manipulated? Stalked? Does this reclusive, lonely rich dude have a crush on me? Why wouldn't he out himself until now? What the fuck is up with my bullshit detector?

Until my feelings are sorted out, I don't want to let him know I'm a little rattled, so I send a simple reply:

"Sure," I type back. "I got you."

Finished with my correspondence, I absentmindedly answer Zara's Spanish Inquisition about my bookkeeping. In between interrogations, we help a few regular customers, and I change up the music and open boxes of new vinyl from the Foo Fighters that have arrived.

I notice Zara is drinking the coffee that Kai has bought for her from Voltaire's and I smile.

I smile a lot more throughout the day as I notice the two of them stealing glances at each other through the plate glass window; Kai outside playing his guitar and Zara inside keeping her fastidious life on track, as always.

I need to execute the next phase of my plan. Sitting at the computer, I pull up a flier I've been working on for a Fourth of July block party fundraiser for the women's shelter in nearby Sand Hill. That shelter took me and Zara in when we had been on the run, and gave us a place to stay while we got on our feet.

This community has been so good to us over the years, it's a way to give back.

If I can get Zara and Kai to work on the block party together, then I can conveniently head out of town, leaving Zara alone with Kai and letting nature take its course.

But first, it's time to celebrate.

THAT NIGHT, Zara actually cracks a beer with me while watching *Plan 9 from Outer Space* (her choice) at the local Brew & View. After that, we roam the boardwalk for a while, talking about her goals, her dreams, her love life. I try to keep the hints about Kai subtle and to a minimum, and she isn't militantly resistant to the mention of his name. With Zara, that's saying a lot.

My head is spinning with the vision of fat grandbabies

toddling around the boardwalk, well before I turn 45. I keep that little dream to myself, though. Some people are appalled at the idea of becoming a grandparent, but there's nothing that would make me happier. It is the perfect start to our Memorial Day weekend.

The next day at work, I spring my plans on Zara, trying to be breezy.

"Hey kiddo, I forgot to tell you, I'm headed up to Santa Barbara to see Marti for a couple of days. I need to recharge and relax on the beach," I say as I move the Doobie Brothers out of "yacht rock" and back into "classic rock." Seriously, this kid and her *categories!*

Did I mention Zara is a tough nut? "Ma, look around you," she says, gesturing out the window. "We have miles of public beachfront access in Sea Grove."

I turn up the volume on Fleetwood Mac. "Yes, but Marti has private beach access. Big difference."

She rolls her beautiful eyes and pushes back some more, giving plenty of valid arguments about why I should stay. But this little tough nut sprang forth from an even tougher nut.

I crank up the volume to the live version of "The Chain," and start to sway around the shop with my eyes closed, going to another place in my mind.

Zara loves it when I do this.

"Fine. Have fun," she huffs.

"You too," I say, snapping out of my reverie to kiss her goodbye on the cheek before I head out to pack. "And could you at least try to lose your virginity while I'm gone?"

"Gross, Ma."

Chapter 5

J^{ed}

TEN YEARS.

Ten grueling years, six albums and six world tours, and I'm finally free. Free from my contract and free from my marriage.

God knows why it took Darlene so long to finally agree to a divorce.

Maybe she was hoping we would reconcile. We tried therapy a couple of times. But there was no use. It always came down to location and tour schedules.

Maybe because she knows how old fashioned I am —I wasn't going to be happy dating someone until the divorce was final. Maybe she was going back and forth in her mind because of her own old-fashioned notions about marriage and divorce.

"It shouldn't be that easy, Jed," she always said whenever I called her to ask her, plead with her to just sign the damn papers.

But we both knew it had been over for more than ten years.

Well, now it was finally over for real, and it was time to relax. I wouldn't necessary say "celebrate." I'm a pretty serious guy, and I'm not one of those guys who gets a celebration cake and goes to a strip club on the night his divorce is final. That's not for me.

I could never erase what we had.

Besides if we had never been married, we'd never have made two awesome kids together. No question about it, Nelson and Watts are the best things we ever did, and she's the world's best mom for them. I would never change that.

So, not celebrating per se, just stretching out my wings, looking forward to meeting the mysterious Dusty over at Galen's house.

When they told me a few days ago that she was stopping by, I decided to gently let the cat out of the bag with her.

It seemed like fate that we were finally going to meet in person. She would be staying a few days, and if we hit it off, all the better.

I didn't have to be back on the road for another three days—plenty of time to see if she found me datable.

I still hadn't told her exactly who I was—first and last name—there's probably no way she would believe me anyway.

I stroll up to the deck, my six-pack of Shiner under my arm. I know it's Dusty's silhouette from a distance against the setting sun. A female in her 40s, asymmetrical wavy hair, Great set of knockers and lots of bangles on her wrists.

Galen introduces us. "Jed, this is our dear friend Dusty. Dusty, this is our neighbor Jed."

She turns to face me, and her golden brown eyes nearly knock me flat on my ass. I feel the need to catch my breath, which at my age could mean a cardiac episode. But it's not that, thank fuck. Because…oh shit. Dusty is not just the lady from the record store. Or the lady with the sexy phone voice.

Instantly, I know she's something else entirely. She's my Dusty. I want her. I have to have her. The heartbreak and angst that have given me a dozen charting blues/rock songs in the past 20 years of my career is all meaningless. It's all a hazy memory in the presence of this…angel. That's what she feels like. Looking into her eyes, everything from my past is healed. In fact, there is no past.

She holds out her hand to shake mine, and her gold bangles clang against each other up and down her wrists, a burned out OzzFest tee-shirt hugging her breasts. Her haircut is the same as in her pictures from the website, but now instead of brown it's dyed all the colors of the rain-bow. A little blue over here, purple over there. She has a beautiful smile and still has the sexy, dusky voice I remember from our 10-second conversation ten years ago. The dirty dog in my brain cannot stop himself from admiring those tits, which are phenomenal up close. I can't help but wonder what they look like without those damn clothes on…even more importantly, what they feel like… taste like…smell like.

I take her hand and it's soft and warm inside both of my big, rough, clumsy mitts. I'm praying she doesn't notice my stupid hands are sweating right now due to my wondering what color her areolas are.

Down, boy. You'll find out soon enough. This chick is a free spirit.

She's also tough little thing, despite her warm, easy smile and her sexy demeanor. Her handshake is firm. Her gaze is piercing and steady.

b

Chapter 6

D usty

"JED from Santa Barbara is Big Daddy?"

My mouth is hanging open. The reclusive neighbor is a fucking rock icon, and I came here to chew him out. My head is spinning.

I want the earth to swallow me up.

He winces at the term Big Daddy.

"I'm sorry, should I not call you that?" I cringe.

He grins. "You may call me whatever you like, pretty young lady," he says.

Well, now. Don't swallow me up just yet, earth. Because I'm already dead from that grin.

He holds my hand a little too long. Holds my gaze with those silvery blue eyes a little too deeply.

I study the face I've stared at on record jackets for much of my adult life, marveling at how none of those images do justice to those kind eyes.

Galen snarks, "He's lying, he hates that nickname."

Jed is staring at me like I'm both the Queen of the Nile and also a piece of meat. I don't hate it. It has been a while since any man has looked at me like that.

Something about his expression is waking up long-dormant sensations between my thighs, tingling my nipples, and sending my heart hammering.

Is this what a groupie feels like?

No, it's more than a star-struck groupie lust.

But don't get ahead of yourself, Dusty. He still messed with your head a little bit for years. Maybe he had a good reason to, but maybe he didn't. Remember who you are.

Jed's sweet, shy smile makes these incredibly sexy crow's feet when his smile reaches his eyes. His salt and pepper hair is close cropped but still has the hint of the long, wild waves he sported when he was a young up-and-comer.

Everyone knows I'm Ozzy's biggest fan. What they don't know is Jed is also near the top of my "list," the list of dudes who—if the universe shifted and I somehow got the chance—would be allowed to rip my panties off in a hot second, no questions asked. No foreplay. No wine and dine necessary.

Marti pipes up with, "Funny story, I think you two may have talked on the phone once or twice and not even realized it."

When neither I nor Jed responds, Galen awkwardly adds, "Yeah, that's right. Hey, Jed. Remember that night you were trying to remember the name of a song, and we called up our friend with the record shop in Sea Grove? Well, this is she. The one with the phenom daughter."

Jed's cheeks turn a little pink.

I bite my lip.

We seem to have a silent agreement not to tell them that we already know.

"It's strange," I reply, without taking my eyes off Jed's lips, "How my record sales spiked after that phone call."

Did I mention Jed is still holding my hand?

I don't really want him to let go. How often in your life do you get to shake the hand of a god? Beyond that, what are the chances that a god is going to continue to squeeze your hand like he doesn't ever want to let go?

One in a trillion.

So, it's OK if I allow myself to feel a little starstruck right now.

Right?

Jed suddenly lets go, and it feels like my soul is going to leap out of my body to follow him.

Just when I feel like the moment is over, he picks up a bottle of Pinot Grigio that's been chilling in Marti's cooler and says, "Dusty, it's time we have a date. Go for a walk with me?"

Oh my god. Oh my god. Oh my god.

My internal organs are having the same reaction as a teenage girl on the *Ed Sullivan Show* upon seeing The Beatles for the first time.

Outside, I'm simply saying yes.

Yes, this is really happening. Yes, I'm going for a stroll with Big Daddy. No big deal.

I try not to let my voice tremble as we make chit-chat while walking up the beach, our bare feet pressing in sync in the hard sand.

Maybe I would look more calm and collected if I would just shut up. But I can't.

"Galen and Marti are in trouble, big time," I say with a wry smile. "I can't believe they've never told me their neighbor was Jed Masters."

"I asked them not to tell anybody," he says, looking a bit sheepish. "I'm sorry."

"You should be, big guy," I say, elbowing Jed in the ribs. It's like elbowing a brick shithouse. "Wow, you're a little beefier than I imagined. Everyone says celebrities always seem shorter in person, but you're taller and…bigger."

"Beefy…that makes me feel like I need to go on a diet," he says with a smirk.

"Don't you dare!" I blurt out, and he laughs.

Oh shit.

"I just mean…I'm pleasantly surprised…despite being mad at you…I'm babbling now."

He chuckles again and the sound reverberates down my spine. "We need some of this wine about now," he rumbles.

Thank god.

"Shit, I don't have a corkscrew, do you?" I say.

"Nope. No keys, either."

"Oh, we can just walk back…" I start to suggest, but I trail off when I see that Jed is removing his belt.

I have no fucking idea what he thinks he's going to do but on the outside chance he's going to tie me up with it, I get a little excited.

Really, Dusty? What's he going to tie you to? A conch shell?

Jed pulls off his belt completely in one smooth move, and the swoosh sound it makes as it slips through the belt loops of his jeans is so hot, the lips of my pussy flutter and contract with lust.

He's going to show me his dick. Do I want to see his dick right now? Too soon? Unconventional, but who am I to question an artist?

Oh but wait.

He's not showing me his dick. He's using the prong of the buckle to screw into the cork.

"There's no way that's going to work… Oh." My jaw drops as he holds the bottle out to me.

"You don't require a wine glass, do you? Because for that, we will have to go back. And I really don't want to go back just yet," he says.

That is the goddamn sexiest move I've ever seen in my fucking life.

He laughs again and I realize I said that out loud. Mortified, I grab the bottle and take a big gulp from it.

"If that's all it takes to get you going, then I've got a lot more where that came from. You should see me open a beer bottle with my nipple," he says with a wink.

I blush as I laugh and hand him the bottle. I have no words.

Walking and fidgeting with my fringy scarf is about all that's keeping me from thinking things that fill me with the overwhelming urge to climb this man like a tree and relieve the delicious ache between my legs.

Compounding my overwhelm is Jed's scent—a mix of cedar and desert sage. Its effect on me is clouding the fact that I should be annoyed with him right now. The spicy, earthy, masculine scent coming off of him, combined with the ocean breeze, is only making me want to dry hump him over top of those sexy, raggedy, boot-cut Levi's.

"God, why do you have to smell so good?" I say, closing my eyes and deeply inhaling as we walk together.

Jed chuckles, with a hint of embarrassment.

"I dunno, you'll have to ask my housekeeper; she puts those essentials oils and shit in the laundry. Maybe that's it."

"Don't ruin the illusion with facts, Jed. Next time a

woman compliments your scent, just say thank you and then maybe kiss her."

Jed stops walking. "Next time? Kiss…her? Her who?"

Busted. He's not going to play that game with me.

"Well, you see…" I start, buying myself some time to decide on what word salad I want to toss right now. JFC, what am I supposed to say? What woman doesn't want to be kissed and pounded by this man? He can take his pick among…all of the women!

"…not that you need pointers on how to pick up women… I just mean if you were interested in kissing me…which you probably aren't, otherwise you would have done something other than emailed me once a week to order records…"

"I am interested," he says.

I'm still walking, but he's just standing there, watching me walk. If I stop and go back, he's for sure going to kiss me.

I turn around and say, "Do I want that? Yes. Do I want a fling with a super-busy rock star? No. I've had ridiculously bad luck in men and I'm not interested in a one-night stand."

When Jed catches up to me, his face has changed. Half of my scarf has fallen off my shoulders in the breeze, and he's catching it and pulling it around me.

"Suppose you tell me all about your bad luck and I'll tell you all about mine," he says, in a gravelly, serious tone that tells me, without the exact words, that he's not interested in a one-night stand either.

Chapter 7

J ed

BY THE TIME we're done sharing our life stories, I'm ready to hunt down Walter myself and make him pay with his own hide.

Making his girlfriend raise a baby with no electricity or running water…not to mention he was probably running around on her, as these charismatic types tend to do. But I didn't float that theory out loud; it would only trigger more anger and it wasn't good for Dusty.

She brings out the protective nature in me that's been displaced for a while now. And it doesn't scare me. Nothing would make me feel more like a man than to stand in the way of anything that would harm Dusty, or her amazing daughter.

"Dusty, I regret not telling you sooner that I was…that I was…"

"My sugar daddy?"

The words punch me the gut.

"I didn't mean to insult you. I wanted to make sure you stayed in business. There aren't enough places in the world like what you have."

She nods. "It's true, I am one of a kind."

She smiles and holds her arms out wide like she's got angel wings. She doesn't need them though; she's already perfect.

"It's a long route to take just to ask me out on a date," she says.

"I wasn't comfortable pursuing something until the divorce was final. It's my own little quirk, I guess. Most people don't get it."

"Jed. Do you even know who you are?" She gapes at me.

"I'm too aware sometimes."

"You can have any woman in the world. You can't tell me you don't have groupies clamoring for you everywhere you go."

I shake my head and take her arm in mine. It's a little presumptuous, but she doesn't pull away. "Nope. Never really got into the groupie scene. Not for me. Too much risk. Too much drama."

Dusty's body stiffens.

"Well, you don't want to get involved with me then. There's probably going to be some drama with Walter getting out soon."

"I can handle his stupid-ass drama," I say, and it comes out a little more aggressive than intended.

"Yeah, but I don't know if you can handle me," she says.

That right there must be my cue to go for it.

All those songs I'd written about love and heartbreak

don't mean a damn thing if I don't press my lips on this deeply sensual woman right this second.

I take a firm hold of her scarf at the opening with both my hands and lean in. Dusty's soft lips sear me like a sparkler on the Fourth of July.

Her skin is soft as petals and scented with jasmine. Dusty doesn't mess around when she decides to kiss someone. She accepts my tongue without urging. The taste of her is better than warm Texas peach cobbler after Sunday dinner. With vanilla ice cream. And a little bit of sea salt just to put everything over the top.

I'm hooked. Immediately.

I'm still clutching her scarf closed, so Dusty's hands finally come to rest on my waist and she hooks her fingers in my belt loops. Like she already owns me. Which she does.

Chapter 8

D usty

JED MASTERS CAN KISS.

This is no surprise.

His lips are as true as his music. Strong and assertive but also full of yearning and heartbreak on a whole other level.

And like his music, he leaves me wanting more.

When our lips part, I breathe in his scent again and count to three to calm myself.

"You seem at a loss for words," he says. "Should I be worried?"

I shake my head. "The fact that you're you and I'm me, and how the hell is this happening to me…it's like feeling very small and insignificant when you're gazing up at the stars, do you know what I mean? It just hits me in waves."

He looks down at the sand and then out at the sea. "Well, It was worth a shot."

I nudge him playfully. "I didn't say you couldn't try again."

I half expect him to laugh again, but instead I've snapped something inside him. He lets go of my scarf and cups my face. He lands a kiss on me that could set my ovaries on fire, if I still had them.

He is just a man. A huge, larger-than-life man with a broad chest that I'd love to straddle and mark with my juice…but still just a man.

My man.

"Wanna take this bottle of wine back to your place?"

Unexpectedly, he stiffens.

I've taken it a step too far, I guess.

"Of course," I say. "What was I thinking? I can't just invite myself over to…"

He protests, "No, Dusty, it's not that, it's more complicated than that."

I know exactly what that means.

When a man says it's complicated, it means I'm potentially a new side piece.

"One second you're a one-woman, old-fashioned man, and the next minute you're something else," I say, backing away. I knew it was too good to be true.

I speed walk back up the beach to re-join the little party that has grown by three or four more people, all the while Jed is following me, full of explanations.

I feel so stupid I don't even want to hear them.

"It's not that I don't want to, it's just that I can't spend the night with someone until I'm married," he says.

I huff, "Well that's a new one."

By the time we reach the party again, there's a bonfire

on the beach and everyone is a little too happy to see their superstar neighbor.

Jed quickly gets imposed upon to grab his guitar and lead an impromptu singalong around the fire.

I beg off, telling Marti that I'm tired and I'm heading off to the guest house.

There's no way I can stay and listen to him play his songs after the way I embarrassed myself.

I'm going to stay in the guest house and then bug out first thing in the morning. Now that the glasses are safely stowed away here, there's no reason for me to linger.

Chapter 9

J ed

I'VE BEEN roped into playing tunes around the bonfire on the beach by the small group of neighbors.

Ordinarily, I would not mind. But I've drunk half a bottle of wine (that I don't really like—I'm much more of a beer man) on an empty stomach, I'm starving but I don't want to eat because I've pissed off my woman.

What I really want to be doing is taking back the last 90 seconds of my conversation with Dusty.

I'm half-heartedly noodling through their requests of some of my songs as well as a few of my choosing. It's all so ingrained in my mind and in my fingers that I actually find myself writing a whole new song in my head while I'm playing another.

The song is making me itch to get the hell out of here.

"Excuse me, Galen, I gotta go take a whizz," I say.

I hear Marti giggle, "She's in the guest house."

But that's not where I'm headed.

I leave behind the Shiner and trudge back to my house with my guitar, picking out the melody on the strings as I go.

When I reach my house, the song is fully formed.

I don't know if it's the right thing to do, and I don't wanna fuck this up.

I gotta try this out on someone else before I play it for Dusty.

So I call up my friend Stephanie.

Some people say she's a goddess, other people say she's a witch. I call her my son Watts's godmother.

She answers on the first ring.

"Hey, Jed, what are you writing?"

This psychic ability of this chick gives me shivers. And not in a sexual way, just in a spooky way.

"Steph, how do you know I'm up late writing music?"

"Because it's midnight and the only reason your old ass is still awake is you're writing a song."

I mumble something about my ass not being as old as her ass.

She laughs. "Your soul is older than mine. Trust me, I've seen it."

"Whenever you talk like that it sorta freaks me out," I say.

"Just play me the song, old man."

I put her on speaker phone so I can strum the chords I've worked out in my head and I sing the lyrics I wrote down in my notebook when I first walked in the door.

When I finish, there is an uncomfortable pause on the other end of the phone.

"You still there?" I ask her.

She replies. "Jed, I'm only going to say this once. Lock that woman down."

"How do you know…"

"Don't be stupid. I know. Something is different. Do you realize you've found your muse?"

My voice cracks. "I do."

"Are you with this woman right now?"

"Not right this second, I'm sure she's asleep…"

"That's not what I mean. Are you committed or does she think you're just fuckin'?"

"We haven't gotten that far."

"Well then why are you wasting your time talking to me? Go to her right now, and unfuck whatever you fucked up. And play her that song. And if she's not yours after that, tell her Stevie sent you. That should work. She's a fan of me."

"How do you know…"

"Jed! Go! Now!."

Chapter 10

D^{usty}

I DREAM I'm in my childhood bedroom at my parents' house.

I've just been grounded for sneaking out to see Walter, an older boy who they deem as nothing but trouble.

I know they're right.

But still, when I hear the pea gravel tinkle and scatter against my bedroom window, I open it.

I let him inside my room, and he's as stealthy as a snake. He convinces me to escape with him out the window. But it's too difficult because suddenly I'm nine months pregnant. I look down in wonder at my belly, but then when I look up again, I'm giving birth in a tent surrounded by strangers. I wake up sucking in my breath in a panic attack. And that's when I realize the tinkling of tiny rocks against a window is not part of the dream. The sound is actually someone tapping on the guest house door.

Oh fuck.

There's no way Walter found me. Has he?

I leave the light off inside and creep over to the window and look over toward the door.

Of course it's not Walter. It's Jed. My heart pounds for a totally different reason.

He's carrying his guitar.

I open the door. "What time is it?"

"I don't know but I got something to say. Can I come in?"

I stand aside and let him in.

We walk over to the bed and I gesture for him to have a seat, because there's not really anywhere else to sit in the guest cottage.

I feel exposed in my baggy tee-shirt and undies. I forgot to pack pajamas, so this is all I have to wear to bed.

I listen as Jed strums his guitar and sings to me.

This is the most surreal experience I've ever had. Big Daddy himself is singing me a song, and I've never heard of it before.

It's about how his hands don't know what to do without me to hold on to. He can't breathe unless the room is full of my perfume. He can't watch another sunset without me next to him.

When the song is finished, I shyly admit I've never heard it before.

"That's because I just wrote it a minute ago."

I laugh. "Wow, how long have I been asleep?"

"Too long if you're sleeping without me. That song is for you, Dusty."

Words fail me.

My heart is pounding but words won't come because my mouth has completely dried up.

"A very smart person told me to get my ass over here and lock you down."

My voice is wavering. "If this isn't real, if this is a dream, I will flat out die."

He says, "I just wanted to let you know I'm dead serious about you, and the reason I hesitated back there is because I've only ever slept with one other woman. Darlene and I waited until we were married. The rock and roll lifestyle never appealed to me. I guess I'm a goody-goody, but nobody believes it. So that's it."

He looks at me and I look back at him. Soon, a smile creeps across both our faces.

I shouldn't be the first to say it. But when the spontaneity hits me, watch out.

"Then let's just get married," I say.

Chapter 11

J ed

"I'M SUPPOSED to be the one to ask that," I say, my chest aching at what Dusty has just said to me.

"Then ask me."

"Fine, I will."

"Do it."

"OK." My knees creak as I slide off the bed and down to one knee.

I take both her hands in mine and I hand her my guitar pick. "I don't got a ring, but I got this. Will you be my wife?"

"I've done crazier things on impulse," she says. "Sure, let's do it."

Chapter 12

D usty

IT FEELS a little weird that Jed only kissed me goodnight and left again.

But Lord I want to marry him. As I meditate on the beach in my tee-shirt and undies the next morning, I suddenly have a massive realization.

"Holy shit, I've never been married before."

It should be obvious, but it's just not something I think about. Since Walter, I've been a serial, casual dater. But ultimately, there was no one I deemed good enough to have an influence on Zara, always my top priority.

The morning breeze on my face is deepening my state of relaxation and making me more certain that I'm doing the right thing.

Hell, I'm 42 and all our kids are grown, it's not like we're ruining anybody's lives if it doesn't work out.

But on some level—all the levels—I know it will.

The smell of salt air is suddenly mixed with cedar and desert sage and all of my senses are aroused. He's here.

My eyes remain closed as I allow myself to enjoy him being nearby. Soon his lips are on my cheeks, my chin, my neck and finally my mouth.

"You're supposed to be getting dressed," he murmurs between kisses.

I chuckle and press my hand to his stubbled cheek. He rubs against my palm and it sends shivers everywhere.

"What do I wear to a city hall wedding at the last minute?"

"Marti's taking care of everything," he says. Before I can stop him, he's scooping me up and carrying me to the house, where Marti is waiting for me in her room with a beautiful summer yellow dress and a bouquet of lavender from her garden.

My friend wraps me in a hug and squeals.

"You're not mad?" I ask.

"Are you kidding? This is all I ever wanted for you."

Chapter 13

J ed

IT'S tough to keep a wedding a secret when you're a celebrity, but I pulled some strings at city hall and I managed to bring a retired magistrate to the house, who witnessed us fill out the proper forms and agreed to marry us on the spot.

It's a beautiful day on the beach, but none of it compares to my bride in her yellow dress with purple flowers in her hair. I'm wearing a white suit with the cuffs rolled up because we're both barefoot.

Galen and Marti have told no one, and they are our sole witnesses.

The ceremony is so quick, I can barely believe it when the magistrate announces us husband and wife.

I'm so happy I can't help but grab her so tight while we kiss that her feet leave the ground. It's easier this way, with her petite frame and my taller and not-so-petite build.

We kiss like that for a while. I'm not sure how much time passes but eventually someone taps me on the shoulder and reminds us we have to sign the certificate.

I can't do it fast enough, because I need to get my bride back to my house.

Our house.

Chapter 14

J^{ed}

I HAVE TO ASK HER.

"Are you disappointed you didn't get a real wedding?"

Dusty is knee deep in my record collection, sitting cross-legged on the floor of my media room, marveling at all the rare vinyl, half of which came from her store.

She looks up at me with a sparkle in her eye. "Did we just get married for real? Then it's a real wedding!"

Her spirit astonishes me. Just being around her makes me feel ten years younger. "Well, yes, you are legally my wife..."

My wife. It's surreal how easy it is to say it.

"I just wondered if you regret not having a big reception with all your friends, most importantly your daughter."

She looks up at me and smiles. "I try not to think too much about regrets."

My heart soars at the knowledge of how perfect she is for me.

"You pick something to set the mood yet, wife?"

"Not yet, I can't decide between 'Darling Nikki' and Justin Timberlake," she says, tapping a finger to her bottom lip thoughtfully.

"How about something a little more old-school?"

She giggles, "Oh my god, those are my old-school picks."

I can't wait any longer to taste her. "That's it." I swiftly hoist her up over my shoulder after grabbing a classic Marvin Gaye album out of the selection she has strewn across the floor, and set it on the turntable before activating the whole-house sound system.

She weighs almost nothing as I carry her, but it could just be because she makes me feel taller and stronger than Hagrid. Yeah, as much as I fucked up as a parent for being away so much, one thing I did correctly was read *Harry Potter* with my kids.

We arrive down the hall at my bedroom—our bedroom—where I gently lay her down on my new California king. Dusty rolls to her side and pets the blankets. "Fancy," she marvels.

I slide up beside her on the comforter and use my fingers to comb her hair from her eyes. "I like you."

"Back atcha," she sighs, tilting her body backward, letting her knees fall open.

This prompts an involuntary growl from my throat. "Don't open your thighs to me unless you plan on squeezing my head while I eat your pussy."

She purrs right into my mouth with a salacious kiss.

"Absolutely, you're going to eat my pussy, but first, something else," she says, her sexy voice going even duskier than I thought possible.

"Anything, darlin'."

"You might think it's weird, but ever since I met you in person, there's something I've been wanting to do."

"What's that?"

"Mark you," she whispers, a pink color rising in her cheeks.

I can be a little dense sometimes, and I say, "We can go get wedding rings tomorrow, if you're talking about outward appearances."

Dusty glances down and bites her lip.

"No, it's not that. Out of nowhere, I just have this crazy urge to mark you, with my juice."

"Oh. OK."

Nobody's ever said this to me before, but hell. If Dusty wants it, Dusty gets it.

"Look, babe, whatever you need to do, let's do it. I've got all night and two more whole days before my next tour date..."

"Lie down," she commands me.

Is there any point in doing anything but what a woman like this tells me to do? I think not.

Seconds later, I'm on my back, still dressed. She has me unbuttoning my dress shirt, opening it wide and exposing my undershirt while she climbs on top of me. She's up on her knees, straddling my hips, unbuckling my belt. Unbuttoning my jeans and unzipping my fly.

She's reaching her hand inside to cup her hands around the bulge in my drawers.

My breath hitches when her hands warm over my cock.

"God. Damn. You're so hard."

"Sweetheart, my pecker has been pitching a tent trying to get at you since I saw you on the deck last night."

"Think you can last a few more minutes?"

"That's one advantage of being my age, I can come on command or not at all or anything in between. You set the pace."

I try to tug my undershirt off, but she stays my hand.

"I told you it's weird. Just hang on."

"OK," I say, not sure what's going to happen next.

What does happen is she starts climbing me like a tree, a tree that's on the ground. She's inching up all the way to my chest, until her pussy is a breath away from my face.

It's not until then that her body starts to buck against me. Her pelvis thrusts against my chest, grinding her pussy on my shirt. It's strange but deeply erotic and I'm all about it.

"Babe, you're so wet I can feel it through shirt."

"Good," she says. "Take it all. Take all of my juice."

"I'd like it better if I could swallow it."

"You will, in a minute. Now, take off your shirt."

She sits up on her knees and gives me room to help me remove my undershirt. She holds it up to my face.

I take a whiff and it smells like some other level of heaven made of Dusty. I can't respond except for a low moan from deep inside my chest.

"I'm going to take this shirt on tour with me and I'm not gonna wash it. It smells like us together. I'm going to sleep with it every night.

"Oh my god, thank you for not thinking I'm weird."

"And every night after a show I'm going to smell it and jerk off, and then fall asleep with it under my pillow."

A wicked smile creeps across her face. "You forgot one part of that equation," she says.

"What's that?"

"The part where you call me while you're doing it so I can hear you come."

"Come here, woman." I wrench her down so I can kiss

her mouth with a thirsty, penetrating tongue, which she accepts with ferocity.

Then I flip her over to the sound of squeals of surprise followed by excited laughter.

My beard gently sandpapers her thigh as I nibble my way across her skin, all the way up to her pussy.

She sighs. "Stroke me with that silver beard, Big Daddy."

I splay open her natural pussy with my fingers, getting a look at her glistening pink sex.

"You're dripping for me, Dusty. It's so beautiful."

I pull back the front of her crevice and easily find her swollen clit. My mouth is watering to taste her.

When I do, it's the sweetest honey I've ever tasted. Like she made it just for me.

I feel her body react at the touch of my mouth, my beard at the center of her. It's a jerk followed by a deliciously wanton thrust. Every lick, every taste, every plunge of my tongue into her sends Dusty pressing her body more firmly into my grateful mouth.

Between kissing, licking, devouring her, I murmur against her labia, "Mine. My pussy. All mine."

With every rumble of my voice vibrating against her tender skin, her moans grow longer, louder, more insistent.

I tease her by giving her a lighter touch with my tongue. Backing out to feather kisses across her milky thighs.

Soon enough her fingers tighten in my hair. "Fuck you, get it done. Don't fuck with a pre-menopausal woman's orgasm, Jed."

"Yes ma'am," I reply and then suction my lips around her clit and suck on it, teasing it with my tongue while massaging her labia with one hand and pushing one finger, two fingers, then three fingers into her sheath.

Her orgasm nearly rattles the windows in this tiny cottage. Her body jerks; she screams; her pussy clamps down; she gushes out yet more of her sweet essence. I'm drunk on her wine.

The fingers she has laced through my hair pull exquisitely at my scalp as she rides the waves of her climax. I suck until she pulls me away from her sensitive core, unable to take much more.

"You're good, a little too good," she breathes as I scoop her up in my arms.

"Nothing's too good for my Dusty," I say, kissing her damp forehead and brushing back some hair out of her face.

Without another word, she's got her hand inside my undies and is pumping me like I didn't just completely zap out all of her energy.

"Babe you don't have to."

"Shh," she says.

Before I know what's happening she's got me in her mouth. Dusty is teasing the tip with her tongue, exploring the ridge under the tip, sucking off the pre-cum with a gratuitous little pop.

"Tastes like candy. You must take good care of yourself."

"I love me a filthy woman who's aiming to ruin me for anyone else."

"I better or I'm not doing my job. Speaking of jobs…"

Dusty blows my mind as I watch her. She licks her palms, takes in as much of me as she can, and uses her hands to get me wet all the way to the base.

She sucks me off like a pro. Like she actually enjoys it.

I never blamed Darlene for not wanting to blow me. This whole time I thought all women hated doing it.

But Dusty…she likes it.

She likes my dick.

"How did I get so goddamn lucky…"

And just as she opens her throat to take more of me in, there's a security alert. Someone is ringing the bell.

Dusty pops off my cock and sits up. "What's that?"

"Don't worry about it, babe, someone's probably just trying to peek through the gate. Happens all the time."

She isn't going to settle back into our wedding night lovemaking until I deal with this. So I check the webcam. But it's not the gate. Someone is ringing the bell at the back door. It's Galen.

There's no way he would ever interrupt this without a good reason.

"Better go see what he wants. Could be an emergency," she says.

I cuss and I grumble as I get up, pulling on some pajama pants. "Emergency or not, he's still going to get a boot up the ass."

Chapter 15

D^{usty}

THERE ARE ABOUT seven voicemails from Zara.

Apparently Marti was going to do me a favor by bringing my things from the guest house over to Jed's. She found my phone, all out of juice, and had been charging it for me. When it came on again, she saw the multiple voice-mail alerts.

I brace myself to listen to them, but I only need to hear the first one to know that all hell has broken loose. The news is not good.

"Walter's out already. And he's been to see Zara…oh man I really fucked up."

I phone her back and it's an ugly scene. She very correctly calls me on the carpet for misleading her about Kai's identity. She's upset that I wasn't there to deal with Walter.

I hang up the phone unable to speak, though I need to get back to Sea Grove immediately.

And then Jed has an irrational idea.

"Let me fly you back to Sea Grove tonight.

"That's crazy," I breathe. "You leave for a tour in two days. You need your sleep.

Besides, how will my car get back?"

"I'll have my drivers take it to you."

I am incredulous. "Drivers…plural?"

"Darlin', I don't play this card a lot, but I'm Jed fucking Masters. I have drivers for my drivers. I'll fly you home on my Beechcraft right now and have my guys drop your car at your place in less than six hours."

I look him in the eyes. "You'd better be really fucking serious about this offer. The faster you can get me home, the better."

"Serious as a heart attack."

We board his aircraft at the small hangar up the road, and we are in the air in moments.

"It's not what I imagined your private plane would be," I say.

"What do you think?"

"The headgear is a nice touch. And the fact that you're flying it yourself is pretty fuckin' hot."

"Oh, did I not mention that I've got my pilot license?" He smirks.

Of course he does.

"It's sort of making me want to finish what I started earlier," I purr into the headset.

"No can do, babe. Too many instruments to do the old-school blowjob while driving trick."

I reach over and put my hand on his thigh. "Oh, but you must be so frustrated that you didn't finish."

He chuckles. "The only thing I'm frustrated about is I don't know when I'm going to see my wife again."

"Really?"

"Really. I told you before I've got Jedi mastery over my orgasms. I'm fine."

I don't believe him. I think he's trying to be polite, but there's no way I'm going to let him land this plane without coming. Not after the brain-shattering pussy-eating marathon back at his house. Our house.

"Dammit, man, you gotta stop wearing belts, this is really slowing me down," I say, scrambling with the buckle.

"Babe..." he starts, but his breath catches when I've already got my naughty little hand down into his drawers. "How soon before we land in Sea Grove?" I ask.

Jed's jaw tightens when I squeeze his cock. "Shit, Dusty... Uhm ... let me just check a minute...about 15 minutes."

Plenty of time for a handy.

With one hand, I lift up my shirt and let him watch me stroke my nipple. I pump him up and down while I talk dirty to him.

"Jed, I cream myself every time I put on one of your records, and that's the truth."

I see him lick his lips and swallow.

"You can still taste me, can't you?"

"Fuck, you've got a filthy mouth."

"You like my filthy mouth," I say, giving him one hard, long, luxuriating thrust with my hand while pinching my own nipple so hard I have to close my eyes and bite my lip.

"Fuck, woman, I'm gonna come so hard in a minute."

"Not yet, Jed, I'm not ready."

"Dusty, are you actually gonna make yourself..."

I hiss as my breath catches with every squeeze, every thrust of my hand on his rock-hard, thick cock. "A single mom finds 40 different ways to make herself come when she needs to."

"You don't deserve that. You're a woman that needs to be properly fucked."

"My pussy was just waiting for you is all."

"Baby, I've gotta start our descent soon and I'll need to concentrate," he huffs.

I start to pump in an earnest rhythm, up and down, squeezing harder and getting my fill of the sensation of his thickness, from the base all the way to the ridged tip that's slick with pre-cum.

He comes ferociously, almost angrily. If I hadn't seen his tender side I might be afraid. When the warm jets of his essence coat my hand and forearms, I'm so happy that I climax along with him.

"Oh Jed, oh god!"

"You don't have to..." he starts.

"Zip it," I say as I continue to massage him until the last of his spasms subside while my sex contracts in titillation. "Just enjoy it."

Moments later, we're on the ground taxiing to a private hangar while we zip up, buckle up and do our best to look presentable.

And now I have to leave my husband and go back to my real life.

The emptiness starts to settle in before the plane is parked.

Chapter 16

J ed

"I'M BRINGING the tour to The Fourth of July fundraiser in Sea Grove."

"But…"

"But nothing," I say to Dusty in the taxi on the way to her flat. "I'm there. There's nothing you can do to keep me away."

When the car stops in front of Vinyl Vixen, I once again claim her mouth while saying goodbye.

"Jed, I can't let you screw up the tour," she says.

"Keep protesting and I'll cancel the whole tour to help you deal with your situation here," he says.

A small tear forms in the corner of her eye and I kiss it away. I then wrap her up in a bear hug and inhale her scent to last me until the next time I see her.

This is going to be absolutely torture.

How the hell am I supposed to go back on tour tomorrow without her?

The only way I know how. Let the misery flow through me and write some new songs with it while I'm the road.

I can think of nothing and nobody else the entire plane ride back to Santa Barbara.

I knew the moment I saw her that I should have gone after her years ago.

I knew as soon as I kissed her that she was mine.

I hate being away from her.

My whole body aches leaving her behind.

It hurts more the farther I fly away.

By the time I fall into bed it's a desperate pain. I need her in my bed. I need to make sure she's OK.

I shouldn't call her up. Guys with game don't call as soon as they get home, do they?

But shit, I'm in my 50s already.

And, shit, we're married. It was so spontaneous, I keep forgetting that fact.

Anyway, if I ever had game it was gone a long time ago.

But first, I think of the perfect wedding gift. I shoot off a text to Stephanie, Watts's godmother. She responds right away. I smile to myself. That was almost too easy.

I dial Dusty's number and she answers right away too, thank god.

"Hey," she says, already knowing it's me.

"Hey, darlin'. Just wanted you to know I got home safe."

An audible, genuinely relieved sigh escapes her. I can't tell you the feeling it gives me what this implies. She was worried.

"Thank you so much for calling to let me know," Dusty says. "It's very thoughtful of you."

"God, I could listen to you talk all day and all night," I tell her.

She pauses a bit. Dammit, I wish I knew what she's thinking. I need to see her face.

"Did I say the wrong thing?"

She laughs, "You said the exactly right thing. I'm just still a little blown away that you would choose me."

I wince a little bit at this. I'm not any more important than anybody else, and the fact that she thinks so will have to be addressed at some point.

"I'm just a decrepit old man with a guitar, no need to put me on a pedestal."

"Say decrepit again and I'll come back up there and smack you. No decrepit old man ever had such a nice, thick dick, I'll tell you that much, Big Daddy."

She makes me laugh and it feels good.

"Can you just come back up here and smack me anyway? Thinking about that kinda turns me on."

She makes this incredibly sexy noise that is somewhere between a sigh and a laugh. "I wish I knew you liked punishment from women a few hours sooner; I could get into that."

I have a pain in my gut at the memory of Darlene and everything we put each other through in the divorce. Before I can stop myself, I chuckle ruefully. "A glutton for punishment. That's me."

Dusty senses something is wrong. "Jed. You know I didn't mean…"

"I know, darlin'. You're good. I miss you already. But I gotta get some sleep and so do you. Just one more thing, I have a surprise for you on the Fourth."

"Just the fact that you want to come is enough. I'll completely understand if your tour doesn't allow it."

"Oh, my manager will allow it or she's fired. It's happening."

It feels good to say that.

Chapter 17

D usty

THIS MIGHT BE the worst pain I've ever felt in my life, and it feels entirely stupid that Jed's not here.

But I can't expect him to help me deal with this mess I've created.

Zara let me have it the minute I came home.

Walter has come and gone AWOL again, but he'd been making threats over having the glasses returned to him.

And now Zara isn't speaking to me or to Kai, because apparently Walter has hired a private investigator and spilled all the beans to her about his past.

So this is some horseshit.

Thank god Kai agrees to stick around and help us deal with Walter if he should show his face again.

In the meantime, things are super awkward around Vinyl Vixen.

The next morning I'm back at work, trying to maintain a stiff upper lip.

I feel a pair of eyes on me as I'm going over the books in the record shop.

I'm pretty sure it's a pair of eyes that look like mine except for they're heavily lined with black kohl.

I look up and smile and my sweet girl. "Hi there. Are you speaking to me again? I missed you, Zara."

"Mom, what's wrong with you? Where's Ozzy?"

I cock my head at my beautiful daughter. "Just because I'm not playing Ozzy on any given morning doesn't mean there's something wrong with me."

"You're playing alt country. You hate that shit," she says.

I feel my cheeks pink and I shrug, unable to control the smile pulling at my lips. "I'm coming around to it."

"Since when?"

"Since I found out Jed Masters has been a longtime customer of our store and he happens to be a big Keith Urban fan," I say with a playful haughtiness, going back to my books.

"Whoa!" I hear from an impressed Kai, who is currently on a ladder and working at removing the hideous drop ceiling and fluorescent light fixtures.

Zara eyes me suspiciously. "Famous people who make music you hate order rare vinyl from us all the time, but you don't turn around and make everyone listen to it."

I shrug again. "Huh, weird."

"Mom, what aren't you telling me? You're the most predictable person I know. I will get it out of you."

I huff and square my shoulders. "Predictable?" I repeat back at her.

"OK, dependable."

"Predictable! Dependable! How dare you!" I am horrified.

Zara laughs. "You know, most mothers appreciate being thought of as dependable, reliable, even predictable."

I stand up and blurt out, "Well, are most moms getting their bell rung on Big Daddy's two-seater plane on a Wednesday night?!"

Zara's mouth falls open. I should not have said that.

Kai is standing there dumbfounded for a beat before he throws his head back and laughs, nearly falling off the ladder. "Holy shit!"

Zara's face is now beet red. "Mom," she grits out. She's totally grossed out and scandalized. "Is that why you went to Santa Barbara at the last minute? To be somebody's groupie like you've always wanted? I mean, I just imagined it would be someone a little more…I don't know…edgy."

I scoff. "You want to talk about edgy? His hands are simply amazing."

"Gross, Ma."

I'm done with this. I don't know where I went wrong with this girl. "Kai, take her for a coffee, I don't need her here this morning."

Zara rolls her eyes. "Kai and I aren't speaking, remember?"

"Fine! Then you get none! Kai, I'll take a large Guatemalan dark roast with a shot of espresso from Voltaire. Black as the deepest level as hell. Please and thank you!"

Zara shoots me a withering look before she retreats back into her obsessive music subcategorizing and cross referencing system.

She can be so uptight sometimes.

Just then, I get a call on the store's land line.

"Vinyl Vixen, this is Dusty."

The voice on the line is a deep baritone, with a rich Texas drawl like smooth whiskey. It burns deliciously before it sends shivers down my spine. "I'm looking for a little darlin' with the sweetest mouth I've ever tasted."

Oh. Shit. I'm already wet. All these shenanigans going on around me and I'm still down to mess around.

"I think she's around here somewhere. Keep talking and she might just come for you."

Jed lets out a growl and the way it falls in my ear, my nipples get instantly hard and my clit twitches.

"I know the kids don't get it, but there is nothing like a landline for having an intimate phone conversation," he says.

His sighs and it gets my heart pounding and my blood rushing to my lower lips.

"By intimate conversation you're talking about phone sex, right?"

"I'm not on speaker, am I?" he asks.

"No," I say teasingly. "And I'm alone in the store for the next little bit." OK, that part's a lie.

In fact, Zara hears me, and indicates with her gestures that she has an errand to run and I'll be on my own in the store for a while. So, not a lie at all.

"Good."

"Why, you gonna make me touch myself?"

"I'm not gonna make you do anything. But I am gonna make you want to do something about that ache between your lower lips."

"That's hot."

He grunts something that almost sounds like frustration and all I want to do is help him get some relief.

The Fourth of July can't come soon enough.

Chapter 18

J ed

THE SOUND of her dusky voice makes my spent cock jerk in excitement. Again.

Yeah, I've just jerked off in the shower and now I'm ready to rumble all over again. I feel like I'm 17, and why am I still doing this fucking tour?

"You ever get dick pics?" I ask her.

"Unfortunately all the time from customers."

The thought of that makes my blood boil and I want to crack the skull of every loser who's ever bothered Dusty. My Dusty.

This also makes me think twice about showing her what I want to show her.

"Certain customers, I wouldn't mind getting a dick pic from. But there is this one who is too much of a gentleman. Too bad," she sighs.

I stay on the landline while I aim my camera phone at my crotch and hit send.

This is the first time I've ever done anything like this in my life. I hope it's worth it.

"You should have one now," I say.

"What? Did you just send me one? That's not fair, my phone is not charged."

"And that, little lady, is your consequence of not keeping your phone juiced up. Call me when you see it after work."

And with that, I hang up.

It pains me to do it, but there's something utterly delicious about it.

And so it goes over the next month, all the way up until I see my wife of the Fourth of July.

All my life, summers fly by in a blink.

This one, until I see my girl again, is endless.

Chapter 19

J^{ed}

IT'S FINALLY HERE.

When my tour bus rolls up into Sea Grove, I'm more proud than ever to know that Dusty is mine.

The entire block party has her signature all over it. Face painting for adults and kids, sword swallowers, art demonstrations, food trucks. And as the sun starts to set there is a group of hula hoopers who actually set fire to their hoops. It's one of the coolest things I've ever seen and sort of makes me sad I don't use hallucinogenics anymore.

But the best part of the entire day is seeing my Dusty.

She's waiting for me as soon as the bus parks behind the main stage.

I lay a kiss on her like I've never laid on anyone before.

As the ocean breeze combined with the smell of cotton candy, popcorn and vegan street tacos fills the air, our lips are sealed together and I don't care if I ever have any of those other things again. Especially not the vegan tacos.

I grip her shoulders and memorize her mouth—part white wine and cinnamon spice.

She sucks in her breath at the intensity of the kiss, and she parts her lips to deepen it.

I cup her face in my hands and sense her body melt into mine. Her full breasts press against my abdomen. Her arms circle my waist and her hands are everywhere.

A small growl escapes me at the feel of her hands on me, the waistband of my jeans, my abs, my rib cage, my chest. She's so hands-on with her kisses and it drives me crazy.

All I want to do is rip off that Ozzy tee-shirt of hers and shred her bra with my teeth.

But there's something else I have to do first.

"Babe, I never told you before, and I want to tell you now, before I forget. I love you. And whatever money you raise for that shelter tonight, I'll match it."

Her eyes widen and her jaw drops. She slaps my chest and hurriedly tells me she has to go make an announcement.

When she's done telling the crowd about the anonymous donor, she drags me out from behind the stage to dance with her.

Kai and Zara are singing and playing together while the crowd pairs off in a sweet slow dance.

"It's our first dance as bride and groom," I murmur in Dusty's ear.

"Oh my god. I forgot to tell you I love you too!" she says, slapping my chest again.

"Ow, woman, I am not in A-fibrillation yet, you don't need to whack my heart to keep it workin'."

She laughs and kisses me again and instructs me to cut it out with the old man jokes.

How can I possibly argue with that?

"So I guess the kids have kissed and made up?" I say.

Dusty looks up onto the stage sappily. "Yeah, I predict grandbabies in about nine months. You good with that?"

I chuckle. "I'm way good with that."

We sway to the music for a while, until I hear Kai playing an original song that just about knocks my socks off.

"I don't know if the kid knows it, but that's gonna be a huge hit. Because I'm gonna buy it from him," I tell Dusty. "Your grandbabies'—our grand babies'—futures are sealed with talent like that."

Dusty sighs. "I don't really want to talk about music right now nearly as much as I want to consummate our marriage."

Chapter 20

D^{usty}

I KNOW what Jed needs to do, and I tell him to go do it. I tell him to go have a talk with Kai about the song while I head up to the flat. I don't need to see fireworks…once you hit the age of 13, you've pretty much seen all there is to see in the fireworks department.

It's been a long day, so I take a shower and smile at my idea to make Zara and Kai run last-minute party errands together to force them to talk. I guess it worked.

When I exit the shower, the bathroom is so full of steam I don't notice the shape of a person in the bathroom door who's been waiting for me.

I suck in my breath when I see the silhouette, because a part of me has been wondering when Walter was going to show up again. I wouldn't put it past him to break into my apartment.

But it's not Jed. It's Zara, and she's shaking.

I wrap her up in a bear hug.

"Hey, hey, hey. What happened? Is it your dad? Is it Walter?"

I hold her by the shoulders and breathe with her until she calms down and tells me everything.

"He's gone."

"Gone, what do you mean, he's gone? He was here and left again? What did he say to you, Zara?"

She swallows hard and spills everything.

Turns out Zara duped Walter into showing up and had alerted the police up north that he had failed to meet the conditions of his parole.

"But there was a scuffle and he ran," she says.

"Oh my god, Zara! Are you hurt?"

She shakes her head no.

"Kai scared him off for good, I think. He's not coming back."

My eyes well up and I hug her again.

Zara comes to her senses and she laughs. "Ma, you're hugging me in a towel and this is super awkward now. I'm going back down to the party."

"Are you sure?"

Jed walks in, and he's heard everything.

"I've already alerted my tour security; they won't hold back if they see him within a block of the party," he says.

I shake my head at. "You really love us," I say.

"You have no idea," he replies, hoisting me up for a kiss.

"Ew. OK. Kai's waiting for me downstairs, I guess I'll see you two … later."

THE DOOR CLICKS SHUT as Zara leaves.

Jed sets me down on the sink.

He leans in and his lips claim me once again. I rub the aching bulge in his jeans.

In the next moment my towel is on the floor.

He has fire and need in his eyes. I moan as Jed presses open my legs and nestles his hips between my thighs. I moan louder when he sinks two fingers into my depth, slicking them up real good.

"Goddamn you're ready for it, aren't you, Dusty."

I laugh. "Get it in me, Jed."

"Let me get a condom…"

"Jeezus no, I had my ovaries removed ages ago. Just do it, man."

That's all the encouragement he needs. He plunges into my pussy.

I gasp. "Oh my god. That's so good."

He rumbles, "Shit. You're fucking tight for me, wife."

"Just for you." I punctuate this with a grip on his cock like a vise. My pussy surrounds him and makes my entire being vibrate with primal pleasure.

"Holy shit." Doing it on the sink is hotter than I ever imagined it would be. And it has everything to do with this scrumptious tree of a man hulking over me, around me, and inside me. He sets fire to every cell in my body. He thrusts into me and I welcome every thrust with a squeal. He wants me and nobody else. He thrusts just a few more times, hard, into me as my thighs squeeze him tight and egg him on.

"Fuck, I'm there. Fuck."

"Yeah, you are, big boy. Put it all in me. I'll take all of it."

I shift my hips and drag my legs up so they rest on Jed's shoulders, allowing him to plow deeper into my pussy.

My body shudders and sweat beads on my forehead.

I reach up to his scruffy chin and kiss him across his lips and then down his throat while he continues to push.

"God, I should have come after you ten years ago."

He keeps his cock sheathed inside of me all the way to the hilt as his fingers find my aching little clit. I gasps when his thumb circles it.

"Oh god. That's good, Jed."

He covers my mouth to drill his tongue into my mouth while he teases my clit.

My legs start to tremble and my back arches.

Jed lets go of everything he's holding back and his cum rushes into me while his throat releases a roar.

"Nobody's ever been this good to me. Nobody's ever made my body feel this way," I breathe while we ride the waves of our combined climaxes.

"You deserve every happiness. I'd like to thank all the damn fools you let you get away," he breathes raggedly into my neck.

Chapter 21

D usty

"I HAVE one more surprise for you, Jed."

The sound and smell of fireworks fill the air as Jed holds my hand.

"I told you I don't really care to see the fireworks, I just want to hang with my husband," I tell him. But he's insisting that we go back downstairs and onto the board-walk to rejoin the party.

We find Zara and Kai and I decide to come clean.

"I'm so proud of you, my girl," I say.

"I love you, Ma," she says, hugging me again. "Thank you for being fully dressed this time."

I clear my throat. "Good, I'm glad you love me. just hold on to that thought because I have something to tell you. Jed and I met and got married in Santa Barbara."

Zara's mouth falls open in disbelief.

"I...what? How... Without me...?"

I cringe. She's hurt. "Yes. I'm sorry. I would have told you earlier, but I wanted to plan a big party for later on, and also you were mad at me, and I wanted to make sure you and Kai were solid before I said anything because I didn't want to bum you out that I was so happy."

I'm babbling again.

"Ma," Zara says. "Don't ever worry about me having FOMO, OK?"

"I don't know what that means, but as long as you and I are good, I'm happy."

"Of course you and I are good," she says, and then with a wicked smile that could only come from a daughter who belongs to me, she turns to Jed.

"Are you my new daddy?"

There's groaning, there's laughter, and then finally Jed has to interrupt and square my shoulders with the stage.

"Now for the real surprise," he says in my ear, giving me a squeeze.

I can't imagine what he's got planned, but then my brain, my mind, my soul, my spirit and the air in my lungs go bye-bye, because on the stage—somehow on my little rinky-dink stage in my teeny little artist colony town —is…her.

"Um, that's…no way. No. Way."

Jed laughs and hugs me from behind. Way."

I open my mouth to make a sound but nothing comes out. All I see is a mass of long blonde hair and black diaphanous scarves and five-inch black heeled boots.

And then she sings. She sings the song that Jed wrote for me.

"What did you do?"

"I called in a favor."

I can do nothing but shake and tremble and cry my fool eyes out as I watch this goddess…there's no other word for her…sing my husband's song. Shake, tremble, weep, and pinch myself.

When it's over, I'm so overcome I don't even hear her call us up on the stage.

Then I realize she's saying my name. "Dusty, I wanted to say thank you for throwing this party. Can you come up here please? Let's all give her a big round of applause…"

I have no idea what's happening anymore. I am outside of my body.

"Also," she continues, "I have been asked to give you this."

The next thing I know, I'm on stage and she's handing me a little blue box.

I'm so confused, and I must look like a complete idiot because she motions behind me.

I turn, and there's Jed, on one knee.

"But we're already married…" I blurt out.

Everyone screams and cheers. A few people are upset that Jed is now spoken for.

"I want to do it again. Marry me and let me give you the great big wedding you deserve."

I look down at the square-cut emerald and white gold ring, and I think my knees might give way.

Then, and always after that, Jed is there to catch me.

Chapter 22

D usty

IT'S OUR WEDDING DAY, and it's a very different ceremony from the first one.

The wedding is again, of course, on the beach. But this time, we are under a white tent to attempt to keep the paparazzi photos to a minimum.

Zara and I only have about 40 guests, all from our little boardwalk community. David and all the baristas from Voltaire, Bennett from the art gallery, everyone from the vegan Greek restaurant, Brody form the surf shop. My parents, who haven't spoken to me since I left to join a commune in the mountains at 21, have decided to come back into our lives. Jed's family from Texas, including his two boys, Watts and Nelson, are there too. Watts's godmother and Nelson's godfather, Willie, are there, and that's enough to cause a stir when the ushers seat them.

It's going to take some time for me to get used to being around famous people.

After the ceremony I go up into Marti and Galen's office to change into a different dress for the reception. Because apparently I'm a billionaire now, and that's just what you do.

I wait there for the photographer to take some quick shots before I meet Jed downstairs to greet everyone at the reception, but he's late.

I dig through my purse to check the time, but of course, my phone is completely dead.

"Fancy party. I guess you won't be needing those glasses now."

I'm so startled I scream and drop my phone and my purse on the floor and freeze.

Walter is standing in the doorway to the hall, with a completely bemused and innocent look on his face.

If I didn't know what he was or who he was, I might think he was just a lost random wedding guest.

"How did you get in here?" I say, trying to keep my voice from shaking. There's no way he got in via the gate to either Jed's or the neighbor's property.

Then he glances down at his jacket and I realize he's dressed just like one of the bartenders.

He puts up his hands innocently "I'm not going to hurt you. I just want what belongs to me," he says.

"I don't have them. They're gone. Somebody already bought them. And then I had to pay them back the money because they were appraised and guess what, Walter, they aren't even the real thing!" All this is, of course, a huge lie. Galen did find an anonymous buyer for the glasses, and we hadn't heard anything about the appraisal. But the bottom line is, they're gone.

"You're lying! Give them to me!"

Because he's shouting now, I hear footsteps running toward us down the hall.

"Yeah, well, I can have you arrested," he says.

"For what?"

"For bigamy! You and I never had a fair division of property when you left."

"Walter, we were never married.

"Common law!"

"You're so dumb you don't even know what that means! Common law is not even recognized in the state of California!"

He's raging now. I've really pissed him off. "Give me the eyeglasses or I will fuck you up, woman."

"I'm gonna fuck you up way worse," says a man's gravelly voice from behind Walter.

Walter and I both look at each other confused for a second.

Then all confusion on my part dissipates when Walter seems to fly backwards through the air.

Next thing I know Walter is on the ground. Jed is standing over him with is foot on his neck.

Walter is writhing around.

"Keep trying to get up, asshole, let's see how fast you break your own neck."

I look up at my mild-mannered, fifty-something husband, and forbid him from ever putting himself down again because of his age.

Epilogue

J^{ed}

WITH ALL OF the excitement at the wedding, Dusty and I decide to take a fairly chill honeymoon.

There's only one place we both want to go, for now: the Rock and Roll Hall of Fame.

As we stroll through the exhibits we talk about how lucky she is that I decided to come look for her before the wedding reception.

"Well, when you didn't have your phone turned on, what else could I do? Everybody was getting mad waiting around for cake," I say.

"So in a weird way, I guess it's a good thing I let my phone die."

I let out a howl of laughter. "Don't get any ideas in that twisted little mind of yours."

She giggles and slips a hand in my shirt and backs me into a dark corner of the museum. "Speaking of twisted, did I tell you how hot it was watching you stand there with your boot on Walter's neck while we waited for the cops to show up?"

I feel my ears turn red. "You did indeed tell me that. In fact, I recall a certain role playing related to that just last night…"

Dusty is on her tippy toes trying to kiss me, but I'm not having it. I grab her and lift her up to meet my mouth, which has become one of my favorite moves.

We kiss like that for a while, forgetting where we are.

All of a sudden, I feel Dusty gasp and break the kiss.

"What is it?" I say, a smirk tugging at my lips.

She's looking white as a sheet and pointing over my shoulder toward one of the exhibits.

I turn to look at where she's pointing.

"Well, how about that." I try to sound surprised.

"It's them. The glasses…those are the same ones…but there's no way…I'm still waiting on the buyer…"

Her gaze locks onto mine. "What did you do?"

I shrug. "Me? Nothing but decide to do the right thing and put an artifact where it belongs. In a museum. The buyer has already put the money for them in your account."

She stares at me, dumbfounded. "The buyer? You? And … they're real? Wait a minute…is this why you wanted to come here for our honeymoon?"

I turn and snap a picture of the glasses in the glass case and then fiddle with my phone a bit, eventually posting them to Facebook, and tagging Walter, who is once again sitting in a jail cell.

Dusty gasps and covers her mouth.

I shrug. "What can I say, I guess I'm feeling petty, after what he did to my girls."

Her eyes sparkle. "I love the petty you," she says, slipping an arm around my neck and kissing my Adam's apple.

"And I just love you," I say, inhaling the scent from her hair. "Always."

83

THE END